THE O'BRIEN BOOK OF
IRISH FAIRY TALES
AND LEGENDS

For Tim
U.L.

For Hugh
S.F.

Published in hardback 1996 by The O'Brien Press Ltd,
12 Terenure Road East, Rathgar, Dublin 6, D06 HD27, Ireland.
Tel: +353 1 4923333; Fax: +353 1 4922777
Email: books@obrien.ie; Website: www.obrien.ie
Reprinted 2002, 2004, 2007.
First published in Great Britain in 1996 by Orchard Books, 96 Leonard Street, London, EC2A 4RH.
This paperback edition first published 2012 by The O'Brien Press Ltd.
Reprinted 2013, 2014, 2015, 2016, 2017, 2018.
The O'Brien Press is a member of Publishing Ireland.

ISBN: 978-1-84717-313-3

11 13 15 14 12
18 20 22 21 19

Printed and bound by Oriental Press, Dubai.
The paper used in this book is produced using pulp from managed forests.

Published in

DUBLIN

UNESCO
City of Literature

THE O'BRIEN BOOK OF
IRISH FAIRY TALES AND LEGENDS

RETOLD BY UNA LEAVY

ILLUSTRATED BY SUSAN FIELD

THE O'BRIEN PRESS
DUBLIN

Contents

✦

INTRODUCTION

I was born in a small town in the west of Ireland and grew up with a great love of books. In them I discovered many of the wonderful stories of Ireland long ago, some of them thousands of years old. There were tales of fairies and giants and heroes, of good and evil, of love and tragedy and fun.

These stories almost seemed to come alive when I went on holiday to my grandmother's farm nearby. There every field had a name and each season brought its own traditions from the distant past. Wandering the fields, it seemed quite possible to discover a fairy under a foxglove or some eerie creature creeping through the twilight . . .

In this collection I have chosen to retell some of the best loved of the traditional Irish stories, and trust that you too will be enchanted by their mystery and magic.

Una Leavy

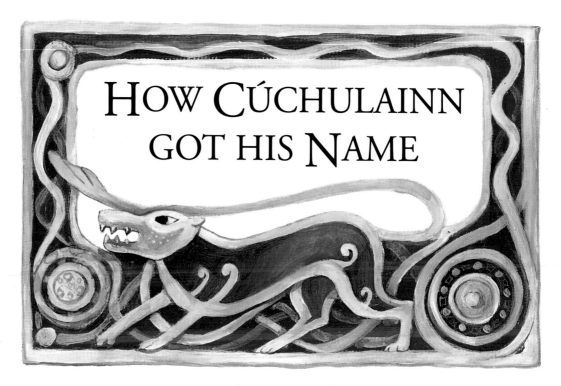

HOW CÚCHULAINN GOT HIS NAME

Long ago, there lived a king in Ulster called Conor Mac Nessa. His warriors were known as the Red Branch Knights. The king himself trained them in his own special school. They could run faster, jump higher and fight more fiercely than anyone else.

The king had a nephew named Setanta. Ever since he was little, the boy had heard about the Red Branch Knights. He could hardly wait to grow up so that he could become one himself.

"I am tall and strong," he said to his mother one day. "I want to go to Ulster to join the Red Branch Knights."

"No, no, my son!" his mother answered. "You are still only a little boy. I cannot let you go. I would miss you too much."

For a while, Setanta was happy. He tracked wild animals in the woods and knew the song of every bird. Sometimes he made hurley sticks from the springy ash wood. He and his friends played together, whacking a ball with their sticks. Setanta's team always won – he hit the ball harder than anyone else and could run like the wind.

A year passed and Setanta grew restless again.

"I am ten years old now," he said to his father one day. "I can run fast and I am very strong. I want to go to Ulster to join the Red Branch Knights."

"No, no, my son!" his father answered. "You are still too young. You must wait until you are older."

For a while, Setanta was content. He milked the cows and kept the sheep from straying. He gathered firewood and carried water for the house. When winter came, there were games of chess that went on for hours. At night he listened to the old people telling their ancient tales.

One autumn evening, a stranger came to the gate.

"I have come from the north," he said, "from the court of Conor Mac Nessa. I seek shelter for the night."

Setanta was delighted. Quickly he took the stranger to his father.

"Of course! You are a thousand times welcome! Come and sit by the fire. We will have music and storytelling this night!"

Soon the house was packed with neighbours and relations. Everyone wanted to hear the traveller's news. All he talked of was King Conor Mac Nessa and his brave warriors. His songs praised them and he recited the history of the king's family for many generations.

Setanta listened, his heart thumping with excitement. In his ears he could hear the roar of battle and the warriors' fearless cries.

"I must go and join the Red Branch Knights!" he burst out at last. "My uncle needs me! I am old enough now! I am strong enough now!"

But the stranger laughed.

"You are only a child!" he said. "You would be smashed to pieces in battle and thrown aside!"

At last everyone settled down for the night. Setanta could not sleep. He lay watching the sparks as they flew up into the darkness and were lost among the stars …

'It's no good,' he thought at last. 'I just can't wait another night.'

Silently he rolled on to his feet, stopping only to pick up his hurley and ball. Outside was the first hushed light of a misty dawn.

All day he travelled, taking directions from the sun. He did not go by the usual paths but kept to remote hills and sheep tracks. Now no one could follow him.

It was evening when he reached King Conor Mac Nessa's fort. Just in front of it swept a great wide lawn. There was a hurling match going on and, almost at once, the ball dropped at Setanta's feet. He scooped it up with his hurley and ran. The players were all big boys. They tried to tackle him but he was too fast, whirling past them till the ball was in the goal!

There was a mighty roar. A row broke out among the boys. Some of them attacked him. Setanta defended himself as well as he could.

"Stop!" shouted the king's voice. "What's happening here? And who is this child?"

"I am your nephew," Setanta replied. "I have come to join the Red Branch Knights."

"Well!" laughed King Conor. "You are only a little man. But if you always fight as bravely, some day you'll be the leader of my army."

So Setanta was allowed to stay.

Setanta soon settled in to his new life. He learned to fight like a stag and to move as silently as the clever red fox. But he learned too about loyalty, honour and truth. Conor was a strict master and only the most promising boys were allowed to remain.

One evening Setanta was hurling with his new friends. King Conor called to him.

"Culann, the blacksmith, has prepared a feast," he explained. "I am going there now. Would you like to come?"

Setanta had heard a lot about Culann. He was as strong as a giant, the greatest blacksmith in the land. He gave wonderful feasts. It would be nice to hear some music and have a little fun.

"I would love to come," Setanta said, "but I am in the middle of a game. I will follow you later – it won't be dark for a long time."

"Very well," said the king, and off he went in his royal chariot.

The game was long and hectic. Setanta quite forgot about the time. The sun was going down when he scored the winning goal.

'I must hurry,' he thought, as he washed and changed. 'It will soon be dark and it's a long walk. I'm not even sure of the way.'

He set off, following the tracks of the chariot wheels. There was no proper road and soon it was almost dark. Trees creaked eerily in the shadows and rocks took on strange shapes. Old tales of ghosts and spirits whispered in his head. Once or twice a wolf howled and owls skimmed overhead. But Setanta would not admit that he was afraid. He whistled a cheerful tune and tried to see how well he could balance his hurley and ball.

It began to rain. A shivery wind trembled in the trees as the last of the light disappeared. Setanta grew cold and wet. He wished he was at home …

✦

Meanwhile, at Culann's house, there was music and dancing. Mead and wine flowed from every cup. Roast pig and fresh oatcakes were piled at every place. The room was smoky and hot. Culann's beautiful sisters tended the guests. The king could not take his eyes off them. As the night went on, he grew sleepy with food and wine. He did not notice the rising wind or the rain that poured down outside.

"It's a terrible night," Culann said. "I will call in my sentries. All my

guests are here. My hound will guard instead. He is a vicious killer and no enemy will enter my gates."

But King Conor was not listening. His eyes were on the beautiful girls ...

❖

At last Setanta saw lights ahead. He was cold, tired and hungry. He could not wait to be inside. He smiled to himself as the noise and music flowed out across the night. The gates were closed but he climbed easily over and dropped into the yard.

Immediately there was a murderous snarl. Setanta stood absolutely still. Two wicked eyes glittered in the shadows – it was Culann's dog, half hound, half wolf! Setanta gripped his hurley. Wild thoughts tumbled through his head. He knew that this dog would eat him alive. There was only one chance ...

As the dog hurtled towards him, eyes raging, mouth snarling, Setanta took careful aim – and rammed the ball down the hound's gaping throat. With a fearful screech, the dog crashed to the ground. Choking and gasping, he tried to cough up the ball, but it was firmly stuck. With one last mighty shudder, he tossed his head and died.

The door crashed open. Culann and King Conor had heard the dog's wild cries.

"My hound!" shouted Culann.

"Setanta!" yelled the king, suddenly remembering. He dashed out, afraid of what he might find. But there was Setanta with the dog dead at his feet.

"I am glad you are safe," said Culann at last, "but I am sad to lose my poor faithful hound. He served me long and well."

Setanta stepped forward.

"I am sorry I had to kill your dog," he said. "But if you will let me, I will be your hound. I will guard your home with my life."

King Conor and Culann agreed. Soon Setanta had another name. He was called Cúchulainn, which means Culann's hound. This was his name, ever after, when he became the best and most famous warrior of the Red Branch Knights.

THE MAGIC SHOES

There was a king long ago called Fergus Crooked-neck. He had once been the handsomest man in the world. But one day he went swimming in a nearby lake, not knowing that a ferocious water monster lived there. The monster attacked, twisting the poor king's neck so badly that it was crooked ever after and no one could make it straight. The king's men failed to capture the monster who lived deep in the centre of the dark, mysterious lake …

At this time, too, there lived another king called Iubdán. His kingdom was the lost, wild valleys between the mountains, and the secret caves of the ancient gods. You see, Iubdán was King of the Leprechauns, and a proud, boastful little fellow he was.

One day Iubdán held a great feast to which all the leprechauns and fairies were invited. There was roast fieldmouse and breast of robin, woodbine honey and elderberry wine. Iubdán sat with his wife, Bébó, smiling at the noise and fun. After a while, he stood up to speak.

"Is this the best feast you have ever had?" he asked.

"It is!" shouted the little people.

"And who is the bravest, cleverest, richest king that ever lived?"

"You are!" they yelled.

The king smirked, till a sniffly laugh rippled from the back of the crowd. King Iubdán flushed.

"Who dares to laugh at me?" he roared.

One of the leprechauns stepped forward. It was Eisirt, the royal poet.

"You!" gasped the king. "Are you saying that I am not the bravest, cleverest, richest king that ever lived?"

"Of course you're not!" Eisirt said calmly. "King Fergus Crooked-neck is greater by far."

"What!" screeched the king. "Traitor! Lock him up! He will be punished for this lie!"

Immediately two guards began to drag Eisirt away.

"Wait! Listen!" shouted Eisirt. "What I say is the truth! King Fergus is a human. His army is ten thousand times greater than ours. Not one of us could carry even one of his gold coins!"

"Rubbish!" shrieked King Iubdán. "Such nonsense – it's nothing but lies!"

"Let me prove it," cried Eisirt. "At least give me one chance to prove that I'm telling the truth."

Now most of the leprechauns liked Eisirt and were sorry to see him in trouble.

"Give him a chance, O King!" someone yelled.

"Yes! Give him a chance! Give Eisirt a chance!" cried the crowd.

"Very well," said King Iubdán then. "You have three days, but if you have lied you will be banished for ever from our world!"

Eisirt prepared for his journey at once, dressing himself in velvet and silk and taking his jewelled sword. Then off he went. The way was long and difficult. Soon the grass made gigantic stalks over his head. Bees seethed in his ear like flying monsters. Sleek, furry paws clawed at him as he passed. But eventually he reached the gates of King Fergus Crooked-neck's fort.

How the guards laughed when they saw the tiny little man! They gladly opened the gates, however, and carried him to the king. With a smile, they set him down on the table between goblets and plates.

The king and his guests stared in disbelief. Then they laughed so hard that Eisirt staggered backwards.

"Have a drink, little man!" someone shouted in a thundering voice.

"No, thank you," replied Eisirt. "I have come to speak to the king."

But a rough hand reached out and dropped him into a cup of wine. Poor Eisirt floundered and spluttered.

"Take me out!" he gasped. "If you do, I will give you knowledge and wisdom." There was a roar of laughter. Now Eisirt was getting angry.

"Did you know, O King, that the bald man sitting beside you cheats you

at chess?" The man gulped, and blushes ran up his neck.

"And that that man with the red beard has stolen money from your treasury? And you yourself, O King, have ... "

But before he could say another word, the king hurriedly lifted Eisirt out of the wine.

At once Eisirt composed a poem, praising the king for his kindness and bravery. King Fergus was very pleased. A pincushion was brought for Eisirt to sit on and he joined in the feast. For two days he remained as a royal guest. But now it was time to return with proof.

"I will send my dwarf Aodh with you," King Fergus said. "He is the smallest person in my kingdom. When your king sees him, he will know you are telling the truth."

So Aodh and Eisirt set off. Now Eisirt rode in Aodh's pocket, giving directions as they went. Eventually a hare came running towards them wearing a golden saddle.

"It's King Iubdán's horse," Eisirt explained. "He will carry us home quickly."

Everyone had gathered to see Eisirt's return. But when they saw the dwarf, they screamed and ran. King Iubdán, however, bravely stayed on his throne.

"This is Aodh," Eisirt announced, "the smallest man in the kingdom of King Fergus Crooked-neck. This is proof that I told the truth. And now, King Iubdán, I challenge you to go there yourself and taste the royal porridge in the king's kitchen."

King Iubdán knew that he would be shamed if he refused.

"I will go at once," he said, "for I am curious to see how these humans live."

"And I will go with you," Queen Bébó declared.

It was nearly night, so, dressing themselves in their mouse-skin robes, away they rode.

All night they travelled on whispering, shadowy paths. The moon faded as they reached the fort and passed the sleeping guards. Through the great wide halls they rode till at last they found the kitchen.

How enormous everything seemed!

A huge porridge pot stood on the table with a gigantic spoon resting on the rim. With a mighty leap, the horse jumped on to the table. But Iubdán was unable to climb up the pot.

"Try standing on the horse's back," suggested Bébó.

Now Iubdán could reach the spoon. He snatched at the handle but, losing his balance, he fell head first into the porridge! Gurgle, murgle, splutter, glup!

"Are you all right?" asked Bébó anxiously.

Before Iubdán could answer, the door opened and in came the servants to prepare breakfast.

"What's this?" boomed a voice. "A tiny man in the porridge! What a messy little fellow he is! And this must be his wife."

"Let's take them to the king. He has always regretted letting go of Eisirt."

King Fergus was delighted when he saw them.

"You will remain here," he said to the pair. "People will come from far and near to see the little people at my court. I will treat you well, but you must not try to escape."

So Iubdán and Bébó remained at King Fergus Crooked-neck's court. They saw for themselves that Eisirt had told the truth. After a while they longed to go home, but there was no chance of escape.

Time passed. The leprechauns were worried about their king and queen. They held a meeting.

"We must go to rescue them," Eisirt said, and he led a mighty army to the gates.

"We want our king and queen," they shouted in their high-pitched voices.

"No!" said King Fergus. "My court is famous since they came. King Iubdán and Queen Bébó will remain here as my guests."

"If you do not let them go, we will scatter all your cattle," said Eisirt then.

"I will not let them go," King Fergus said.

"We will poison all the water."

"I will not let them go."

"We will burn each mill and storehouse."

"I will not let them go."

"We will flatten all your corn."

"I will not let them go."

"If you do not release them, we will make all your people bald – every man, every woman and all your little children."

"If you do that," said King Fergus angrily, "you will never see your king and queen again!"

Then Iubdán asked to speak to his people.

"You must not cause any trouble," he said. "Go home peacefully. King Fergus and I will sort this out ourselves."

So, grumbling and grousing, the little folk returned home.

"Now," said King Iubdán, "you see that my people are very angry. You may have any of my treasures if you release myself and Bébó."

And Iubdán showed his wonderful possessions: a spear that always hit the target, a belt that prevented sickness, a cauldron that was never empty and a pair of magic shoes that could walk on water.

King Fergus thought for a moment, then he smiled. "I'll take the shoes," he said. "If they prove their magic, you will both be free to go."

Of course, the shoes were tiny, but they stretched to fit. Then, taking his sword, King Fergus set out for the nearby lake. The day was still and his reflection shimmered in the water. The sight of his crooked neck filled him with rage. Putting on the magic shoes, he stepped lightly over the water.

There, in the centre, the monster lay asleep. Fergus dived, plunging with his sword. At once a fountain of blood shot into the air. There was a wild struggle. The monster lashed and thrashed, but the king was faster. He skipped across the waves, thrusting and cutting as the monster appeared. With one last rush, Fergus swiped off the creature's head. To his great surprise, his own neck was immediately straight and all the people watching him clapped and cheered ...

And so King Iubdán and Queen Bébó were released. There was feasting and dancing till the next new moon. Iubdán couldn't quite help boasting a little about his great escape, but he never ate porridge after that.

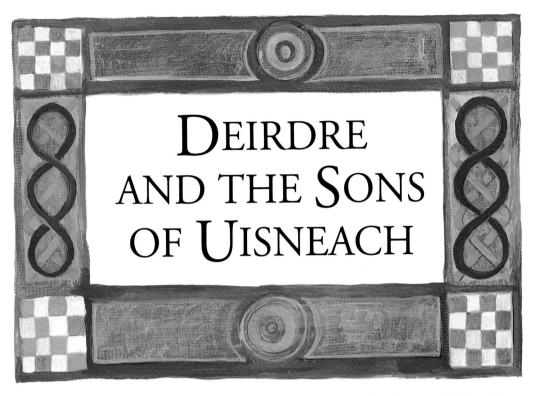

DEIRDRE AND THE SONS OF UISNEACH

A baby girl looked up out of her cradle and yawned. She curled her fist around her nurse's finger.

"Poor little creature," murmured the nurse. "What will become of her?"

In the next room, a fierce argument was going on.

"Let the king decide!" someone was shouting.

"The king can do nothing!" yelled another.

"The stars never lie!" bellowed a third.

"Here is the king now," said the little girl's father. "We will ask his advice."

"What is the matter?" asked King Conor. "Why is everyone shouting?"

The chief druid stepped forward.

"There is terrible news, O King," he said. "We have looked at the stars to see this baby's future. She will bring bloodshed and war. And though she will be the most beautiful of women, thousands will die because of her."

"Let us kill her at once!" someone roared.

"No, please!" cried the father. "What harm can she do? She is only a little baby!"

King Conor thought for a moment. At last he spoke.

"This child will be hidden away," he said. "Her nurse will take care of her and no one else must ever see her. When she grows up, I will marry her myself. There will be no wars because of her."

Everybody agreed to the king's plan. Little Deirdre was taken away to a small house in the forest, with her nurse, Leabharcham, to mind her.

Years passed. Deirdre began to grow up. There was no one to play with and she was often bored. To pass the time, Leabharcham told her stories of the outside world. More and more, the poor girl longed to escape.

"You must stay here in the forest," her nurse warned. "Some day King

Conor will come and take you to his fort. You will be his bride and have everything you could wish for."

"Is the king handsome?" Deirdre asked.

"I really couldn't say," Leabharcham replied. But she looked at Deirdre sadly. King Conor must be old by now while Deirdre was so young and already beautiful.

One snowy winter morning, Deirdre was wandering among the trees. Everything was white and still. Suddenly she noticed a blackbird trapped in some briars. As she reached in to free him, she cut herself on the thorns.

"There is only one man I will love," she said to her nurse. "His hair must be dark as the blackbird's wing, his skin white as the snow and his cheeks red as the drops of blood on my finger."

Without thinking, Leabharcham replied, "Naoise, son of Uisneach, is the only such man in the world."

"Then let me see him!" Deirdre cried. "Please, Leabharcham, I'm so lonely! Please let me see him just once!"

"Poor girl," thought the nurse. "She's had such a sad life. What harm can one meeting do?"

So, wrapping her cloak tightly about her, she set off to find Naoise.

All that long day, Deirdre waited. She tidied the house, walked in the woods, followed the tracks of the birds. But it was so cold! Snow drifted in hollows and darkness came early. She returned to the house and built up the fire. Again and again she looked out of the window. Would they never come? Maybe they were lost in a snowdrift … At last, worn out with worry, she fell asleep.

"Deirdre!"

Someone was calling her name. She opened her eyes. A man stood in the firelight. His hair was dark as a blackbird's wing, his skin white as snow and his cheeks red as drops of blood …

"Naoise!" she whispered.

And Leabharcham watched helplessly as they fell in love.

"I will never marry Conor," said Deirdre next day. "I only want to be with you, Naoise. Please take me with you! We will go far away, where the king cannot reach us."

"Very well," Naoise replied. "But my two brothers must come also. They will help to protect us."

So Deirdre and the sons of Uisneach set off into the cold winter world. They went to all the kingdoms of Ireland. But though they were welcomed everywhere they could not stay long in one place. King Conor had sworn revenge.

"I will follow them to the world's end!" he roared when he heard what had happened. "I will kill the sons of Uisneach and Deirdre will be mine!"

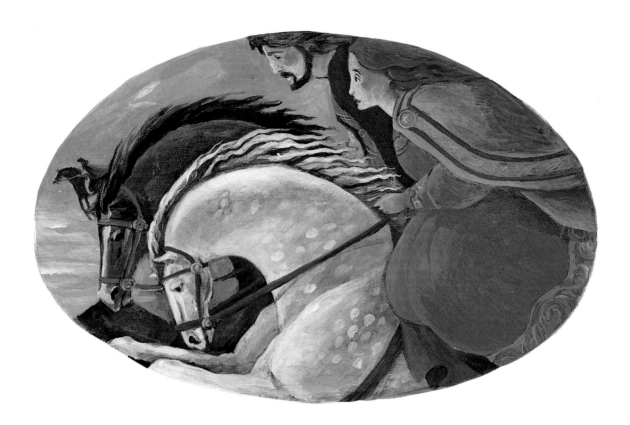

And he sent out his best trackers and hounds.

The dogs roamed the country. Night and day they tracked the lovers, tracing their scent through snowbound valleys and frosty forests. Now their howling rang clearly through the mountains.

"Hurry! Hurry!" cried the brothers. "We must ride faster. Conor's men are just behind us!"

The faithful horses charged bravely forwards, over a hill – and there before them was a great stretch of water.

"We are trapped!" cried Deirdre. "Look! There is the sea! We can go no further! Oh, Naoise! Naoise!"

"And there is a boat!" shouted Naoise. "Quickly, Deirdre, there's hope for us yet! Over there is the coast of Scotland!"

Somehow they stumbled into the water, scrambling on to the boat as it floated out on the tide. Hungry and exhausted, they set sail for Scotland while the hounds howled on the shore.

The King of Scotland heard of their arrival. He sent for them at once, but as soon as he saw how beautiful Deirdre was, he fell madly in love with her. During the evening he spoke to her.

"Stay here and be my wife," he said. "I will give you gold and jewels. You will be Queen of Scotland and have all you could wish for."

But Deirdre loved only Naoise. When night came she crept away with him into the freezing misty darkness ...

All night they wandered, not knowing where they were going. When morning came, they were near the sea again, and there on the horizon was an island. Once more, they set sail. The island was small but Naoise and his brothers quickly built a shelter.

Now, Deirdre and Naoise settled into their new life. The harsh winter passed. Spring came, speckled green and yellow. The great wide sky swept clear and clean over their island home.

Deirdre was delighted. She was free at last, running with Naoise along the shore or climbing the sun-dappled hills. She filled their little hut with sprays of hazel and primroses. When the brothers were fishing or

hunting, she cooked and cleaned. At night they sat around the fire, telling the day's adventures and talking of times past. Though Naoise loved Deirdre more than ever, he missed his home and friends. But he did not tell her.

The year passed and autumn came. Now the nights were getting a little longer. One evening, as Naoise went to close the door, someone was standing there.

"Naoise, son of Uisneach, is it you?" called a voice.

"Fergus! My dear friend Fergus!" Naoise cried. "Come in! Come in! It's great to see you! Come in to the fire!"

Fergus had just sailed from Ireland. He had important news.

"King Conor has forgiven you!" he smiled. "He wants you to come home. He sent me specially to tell you!"

"Wonderful!" cried Naoise. "You don't know how I've longed for this news!"

But Deirdre shook her head. "Don't go, Naoise," she cried. "I don't trust the king – he will kill you!"

"Nonsense!" laughed Naoise. "The king is getting old. All this running around is bad for his health."

"Please, Naoise," Deirdre said. "If we return, something terrible will happen."

"Don't worry, Deirdre," said Fergus, "my sons and I will protect you. Naoise would like to go back – he's homesick."

"Please, Naoise, don't go!" Deirdre begged once more.

But Naoise just kissed her and told her not to worry ...

They left next morning. Deirdre paused at the door. One last spark glittered on the hearth. Sunbeams drifted gently across the floor ...

Soon the boat was sailing west.

"Don't cry, Deirdre," Naoise said. "Soon we'll be home. Everything will be all right." But he could not comfort her.

They reached Ireland. Naoise and his brothers were excited. They could hardly wait to land. But, once more, Deirdre tried to change their minds.

"Please, Naoise," she begged. "If you love me, don't land. Let us go back to Scotland before it is too late."

But again Naoise kissed her, saying, "Don't be afraid, nothing will harm you."

There was a messenger from King Conor on the shore.

"You are welcome," he said. "The king has asked you to his fort at once. You, Fergus, have been invited to a harvest feast. But I will take the guests to the fort myself."

"It's a trick!" cried Deirdre. "King Conor doesn't want Fergus to be with us. Don't trust him!"

"Don't worry," Fergus replied. "I must go to the feast, since it would be rude to refuse. But I will send my two sons to guard you."

So Deirdre and Naoise and their followers set out for King Conor's fort. Deirdre's face was pale and her hands trembled on the reins.

But Naoise laughed and joked. "Cheer up, Deirdre!" he said. "We're home! We'll build a fine house and fill it with flowers."

But Deirdre could only think of the little hut where she'd been so content.

At the fort, the king's army was waiting to welcome them. One of the chieftains stepped forward and spoke to Naoise.

"I greet you in the name of King Conor," he said – and thrust a knife straight into Naoise's heart!

With a wild cry, the sons of Uisneach and the sons of Fergus lashed out with their spears and a vicious battle began. Deirdre cradled Naoise's body

in her arms amid the fighting throng. Someone snatched her away. All night she heard the screams of battle and the clash of spears, but nothing mattered any more. Naoise was dead, she would never see him again ...

By morning, it was all over. Fergus, returning from the feast, found a thousand warriors slaughtered on the blood-soaked lawns. And there among them were the sons of Uisneach and his own two sons. Screaming with rage and grief, he vowed revenge on the king who had betrayed him. For seven years, he attacked the kingdom of Conor, so that thousands of warriors were slain and the rivers flooded with blood.

As for Deirdre, she could not sleep or eat. She never spoke again and within a few months she too was dead. They buried her with Naoise and his brothers – poor, beautiful Deirdre of the sorrows.

❖

The druids were right. Not even a king could change the message of the stars ...

THE KING'S SECRET

There were once two friends named Shane and Éanna. They lived in a village at the foot of the Ox Mountains. Shane was a harper at the king's fort while Éanna was a barber and cut people's hair.

The king lived in a nearby valley. Labhraidh Loingseach was his name and everyone admired him, for he was handsome and brave. He was kind to his people, helping anyone in need. But something was wrong. The king had a strange secret.

"Why does he always keep his head covered?" people asked. "Even when he's swimming, he wears a linen cap."

"And that's not the worst bit!" they whispered. "It must be a dreadful secret, for every time he gets his hair cut, the barber is put to death!"

"Who will be next to cut the king's hair?" worried the barbers, for there were very few of them left.

Now Éanna's mother was a widow. She was always afraid that the king would send for her son.

"You must go away from here," she told him. "How many barbers have already been killed? The king will surely hear of you and next time it could be your turn."

"I'll never leave here," Éanna said.

He looked out at the clouds that shadowed the mountains.

"My father was born here, and his father before him. Not even the king is going to force me away!"

But not long after, the dreaded message came. A servant rode up to the barbershop door.

"King Labhraidh Loingseach orders you to his fort tomorrow at noon."

"What will I do?" cried Éanna to Shane. "If I cut his hair, I will surely die and what will my mother do then?"

"The king is expecting the Princess Aisling to visit him soon," said Shane. "That's why he wants his hair cut. If only we knew what to do!"

But though they plotted and schemed, they could not think of a plan.

"You must go away in the night!" cried Éanna's mother when she heard. "Dress up in my old clothes – people will think you're a poor woman of the roads."

"I will not run away!" Éanna said. "I'll go to the fort and face the king."

Next day, Éanna set out on his journey. He wore his best clothes and his only pair of boots. His scissors, polished and sharpened, were strapped in a little case. At doors and windows faces whispered and stared. One or two called out, "Good luck, Éanna!" But most of them thought, 'Poor fellow! We'll never see him again.'

At the fort, Éanna was shown into a room. In spite of his fear, he just stared and stared. Such colours! Such carvings! Such hangings and antlers and rugs!

The king came in. He nodded to Éanna, then sat in his royal chair.

"Begin," he said, as he reached up to take off his crown.

But what was that huffle and scuffle outside? The door crashed open and Éanna's mother came tumbling in!

"I'm sorry, O King," said the guard. "This woman pushed right past me. She demanded to see you. I'll put her out at once."

The king frowned but the woman threw herself at his feet.

"Your majesty!" she said. "I am a poor widow, and this barber you sent for is my only son. I beg you, please do not kill him. If he dies, it will kill me as well!"

King Labhraidh Loingseach looked down at the old grey head. Something stirred inside him, for he was really a kind man.

"Very well," he said at last. "I will not have him killed. But he must promise not to tell anyone what he will see in this room."

"I promise!" Éanna gasped.

❖

When Éanna came home, his mother asked no questions. She gave him a plate of boxty and a mug of buttermilk. In the evening Shane called and the friends went fishing as usual in Lough Talt ...

Word soon spread that Éanna was alive and well. Next morning the little barbershop was packed to the door. Suddenly everybody wanted a haircut, including some who had no hair at all! But Éanna kept his mouth shut. Snip, snap, snip went the scissors and that was all anybody heard.

Time passed and Éanna found the secret harder and harder to keep. Day after day he thought about it, until he could think of nothing else. He closed his shop early and opened late. One day he didn't open it at all. And though customers called, there was only his mother to be seen.

"Éanna's not well," she said. "Please come some other time."

It was true – now Éanna could not eat or sleep. He grew pale and thin. His mother was half crazy with worrying.

"See," she said, "I've baked fresh bread. And here's honey from the mountain bees. Eat now and you'll soon be well again."

But he could not touch the food.

At night he shivered in bed. He saw each star that came and every wisp of cloud crossing the moon. His mother sang to him but it was no use. Soon he could not leave the house. He sat watching the sparks on the hearth and looking into the flames. The king's secret haunted him.

Shane missed his friend. There were no more rambles in the mountains, no more seeking for trout in Lough Talt.

'Something will have to be done,' he thought. He went to see the druid, a wise man who lived in distant woods.

"I cannot help him," said the druid. "He must tell his secret to someone, then he will be well again."

"But he promised the king!" Shane groaned.

"Well," said the druid, "there's only one thing to be done. Send him to the stream near the king's fort. There is a willow tree leaning over the water, with reeds growing in its shade. If he tells his secret to the reeds, all will be well."

Shane hurried back with the druid's advice. At once Éanna went to the stream. He knelt on the mossy stones, and under the willow tree he whispered his secret to the reeds:

"King Labhraidh Loingseach has horse's ears!"

At once a great weight lifted from him. He went home and opened up his little shop. When evening came, he ate four duck's eggs for supper. And he was fast asleep before his mother could quench the lamp ...

That night a soft wind blew from the west. In the stream, the reeds bent and swayed. They began to murmur to one another. The wind listened and whistled in the willow tree:

"Labhraidh Loingseach has horse's ears!
Labhraidh Loingseach has horse's ears!"

Soon the whole wood was whispering with the news ...

"Labhraidh Loingseach has horse's ears!
Labhraidh Loingseach has horse's ears!"

A few days later the king awoke early. A messenger was galloping up to the fort gates.

"The Princess Aisling is coming today!" King Labhraidh Loingseach jumped from his bed. There was so much to do!

All morning the place was in a scurry. A great fire was lighted in the kitchen. Pigs roasted, cakes baked, servants hurried back and forth. The king sent for Shane.

"Tonight you must play your best and merriest," he said. "I am going to ask the princess to marry me and nothing must go wrong."

Shane went and took out his harp. He examined it carefully, turning it this way and that. He was not satisfied.

"The wood is cracked," he thought. "If I hurry, I can make another harp before night."

He went at once to look for wood. There was the willow tree leaning over the stream, with reeds growing in its shade.

"Just what I need," said Shane, sawing off a branch. All afternoon he worked, shaping and carving the smooth, beautiful wood. At last the harp was made. Carefully he put in the strings but there was no time to

test it – Princess Aisling was already at the gates.

A great feast was prepared. The king led Princess Aisling to her place.

"How handsome he is!" she thought. "But I have heard such strange tales! Some say he is kind, and others that he's evil and cruel. There's some mystery about him – oh, I wish I knew!"

The king could not stop looking at the princess – such beautiful eyes, such wonderful hair! But she seemed worried and sad. She sat pushing the food around her plate.

"Bring on the harper!" cried the king. "Let's have a little merriment!"

Shane took up his harp. But instead of music, there was a rustling wind. It swept around the great hall and rose to the smoky roof:

"Labhraidh Loingseach has horse's ears!
Labhraidh Loingseach has horse's ears!"

Horrified, Shane muffled the harp. But it was too late. Nobody stirred. Nobody spoke. The only sound was the great log fire spluttering in the grate.

Princess Aisling's cheeks grew pink. She gave a tiny snort, then a little chuckle, then a great big laugh. She laughed and laughed. All at once, the whole court burst out laughing.

"Ha ha ha ha ha!" they bellowed. "Labhraidh Loingseach has horse's ears! Labhraidh Loingseach has horse's ears!"

The king grew red.

'What a silly secret,' he thought to himself, 'and what a silly fool I am. It doesn't matter. Nobody cares!'

Then, taking off his crown, he showed them his ears.

And that was that. The king was never again ashamed of his ears. Shane got three kisses from the Princess Aisling and Éanna cut the king's hair for the royal wedding!

THE CHILDREN OF LIR

There was once a race of people in Ireland called the Tuatha Dé Danann. They knew about magic and casting spells. One of them, Lir, was a king. He lived happily with his wife and four children.

One dreadful day his wife became ill and died. Lir and the children were heartbroken.

"Don't worry, Father," his daughter, Finnuala, said some time later. "I will look after my little brothers."

"You are too young," said Lir gently. "Children need a mother. Some day I will marry again."

One day in summer, Lir had a visitor. It was Aoife, his wife's sister. She hugged the children and smiled at Lir. Her eyes were dark as elderberries, her skin creamy as milk.

"It's such a sunny day," she said. "Let's eat outside. You must not be sad any more."

The children were delighted and Lir fell in love with her at once. Aoife would make a perfect wife and mother ...

Aoife too was pleased.

'My plan is working,' she thought. 'Soon I will be queen. Lir is rich and will give me anything I ask for. But those children are a nuisance. When we are married, I will get rid of them.'

A sudden wind howled round the fort and clouds buried the sun ...

Soon there was a royal wedding. It lasted for days, then Lir and his bride travelled the kingdom.

"How beautiful his wife is!" people said.

But one old man shook his head.

"Haven't you noticed?" he asked. "Wherever she walks, the wind howls, and clouds bury the sun. This woman will bring trouble."

But they only laughed at him.

"Don't be silly! It's just the weather!" they said.

At last Lir and his new wife returned home. Aoife went inside to try on her new jewels and robes. Lir walked contentedly outside his fort. His four children were playing on the lawn.

'How good they are,' he thought to himself, 'and how quickly they are growing! I must spend more time with them.'

So every day after that he played with the children – and spent a little less time with his wife.

Aoife noticed. She began to get restless. She did not enjoy swimming or fishing with the children. She felt bored and left out. Lir was rich – he could go anywhere, get anything he wanted. Why did she have to stay at home while he rambled off on stupid adventures with those children? Lir loved them, that was why, maybe more than he loved Aoife.

As time went on, Aoife grew more and more jealous.

'Only for the children,' she thought, 'I would have Lir all to myself. I must get rid of them.'

One day, she spoke sweetly to her husband.

"My dear," she said, "the children are growing up now and don't need us. It will be good for them to go away from home. We can have such wonderful times together, just the two of us."

"No, Aoife," Lir replied. "Those children are part of me. I would die without them."

Time after time she tried to persuade him, but it was no use.

Aoife became desperate. A terrible idea took hold in her head. It choked her heart and smothered her brain, until one day she thought of a dreadful plan ...

It was summer. All was still in the drowsy heat. Lir dozed in a shady corner as Aoife called to him.

"I am taking the children to swim in the lake. It is so warm."

Lir was pleased. He had begun to think lately that Aoife was not

completely happy. She hadn't played with the children for such a long time. Lazily waving goodbye, he settled down for a snooze ...

The children enjoyed the chariot ride. Soon they were tumbling down the hill and into the lake. Laughing and splashing, they chased each other in the cool fresh water. Heat shimmered in the bushes across the lake. Everything was still – it was too hot even for the birds.

Suddenly Aoife, lifting up her arms, began to chant strange words. The sun darkened, a chill wind whipped over the waves. Finnuala watched uneasily. She turned to her brothers, but they were staring at her in horror.

"Finnuala! Your hair! What's happening to your hair?"

Finnuala looked down. Her long dark hair no longer swirled around her in the water. Even as she looked, white feathers grew over her shoulders covering her skin, and in place of her arms were two wings!

Too frightened to scream, Finnuala looked back at her brothers. She was just in time to see their rosy cheeks disappear as they too were covered in smooth white feathers. Finnuala and her brothers had been changed into swans!

There was a mighty clap of thunder. Spears of rain lashed around her, but Aoife didn't care. Her spell had succeeded – now she had nothing to fear!

Then one of the swans began to speak, for Aoife's magic had failed to destroy their voices.

"What have you done to us?" Finnuala cried. "Why have you done this wicked deed?"

Aoife laughed.

"Lir is mine now, all mine!" she screeched. "And you – you will remain as swans for nine hundred years! You will spend the first three hundred on this lake, three hundred in the Sea of Moyle and the last three hundred on Inish Glora in the west. You will never be human again until you hear the sound of a holy man's bell! Now get away from here! I will never have to look at you again!"

And though the swans called to her and begged her to have pity on them, she would not listen. She climbed up the hill by Lough Derravarragh and hurried away.

The sun shone again, the water lapped gently on the shore, but

Finnuala and her brothers could only huddle together. They tried to comfort each other.

"Our father will save us," Finnuala said. "You know how much he loves us. He has all the powers of the Tuatha Dé Danann. Don't cry, little brothers, we will soon be home again."

❖

When she reached the fort, Aoife tiptoed over to the sleeping Lir and gently kissed him.

"Wake up, Lir dear," she said. "I have sad news. Your four children drowned in the lake. But don't fret – I will take care of you. Now we are alone at last ..."

"Drowned! How? What ... what happened? Oh, my children! My children!"

And flinging Aoife aside, Lir ran like a madman towards the lake, yelling their names, gasping and sobbing. But when he reached it, there was nothing to be seen except the softly lapping water ... and four swans.

Lir threw himself to the ground, rocking back and forth in sorrow and despair. Then a voice spoke to him.

"Father, don't grieve. We are not dead. Aoife has changed us into swans. It is Finnuala who speaks."

Lifting his head, Lir almost forgot

to breathe as the biggest swan told him of his wife's evil deed.

"Oh, my children!" he cried. "My poor beautiful children! But don't despair. I will make Aoife take back this wicked spell. Stay here – I will soon be back."

And he rushed off to the fort.

Aoife sat calmly brushing her hair.

"What have you done?" cried Lir, shaking her by the shoulders. "Are you crazy? You know how much I love those children. How could you do such a thing? Come at once and take back that wicked spell!"

"No, Lir," Aoife replied. "You are all mine now. Your children have gone – who cares about a few swans?"

Lir begged and pleaded and threatened and screamed, but Aoife went on brushing her beautiful hair.

Then Lir called on the powers of his god-ancestors and in a terrifying rage he changed Aoife into a demon. With a terrible screech, she vanished into the air, leaving only a trickle of ashes and the stench of burning hair ...

Lir rushed back to the shore and told the children all that had happened. And though he tried and tried, he could not free them from Aoife's awful spell. He cried as he touched them, stroking their feathers. Now there was no power on earth that could save them.

All that long day, Lir stayed on the shore and when night came he would not go home. "You will get cold," his servants said. "And it looks like rain. Tomorrow you can come again."

But he would not leave. So they built a little fire to keep him warm. Friends came to keep him company, for the news had spread. When morning came, more and more people arrived to comfort Lir – and some just to stare ...

Eventually Lir had a hut built on the shore. He slept here at night and spent every day with the swans. He mourned for his children, but at least he could speak with them.

Years passed. Lir grew old. One wet winter day he caught cold. His poor tired heart could not take any more and he died. The swans were heartbroken. In time, the hut rotted away and people stopped coming to the lake.

Winters came and went. All the time, Finnuala cared for her brothers and tried to keep them cheerful and brave.

At last, three hundred years were over. The people who had known Lir and his children were long since dead. One morning, the swans left the lake and flew north to the Sea of Moyle. Only one little girl, looking upwards, wondered if they were the children of Lir ...

The Sea of Moyle was harsh and wild. North winds lashed with icy splinters, snow whirled so fast that the swans could scarcely see. Time after time, they were dashed apart, their feathers stiff with ice. Winter gales hurtled them towards sharpened rocks. But, whenever she could, Finnuala kept her brothers under her wings, singing to them the songs they knew when they were children. She reminded them of happy times that were past and the wonderful days they had spent with their father. And somehow they survived those three hundred long, bitter years.

When their time was up, the swans gladly flew south-west. They landed on the island of Inish Glora. The wild Atlantic was rough and cold, but nothing could be worse than what they had already endured.

Here, summer brought gentle winds and sunshine to warm their bones. By now the swans were tired and old. They had almost forgotten how to speak. Still Finnuala encouraged them and reminded them of Aoife's words – that, one day, they would be set free by the sound of a holy man's bell …

And so the time went on. One evening as the sun set, Finnuala lifted her head, listening. Yes, there it was again – the clear, sweet ringing of a bell.

"Surely this is the sound we have been waiting for!" she cried. "Let's go ashore at once!"

They stumbled on to the strand. Clumsily they climbed up a steep grassy path to a group of stone huts. A man came out. He was surprised to see swans at his door, but when Finnuala spoke he staggered back!

"Don't go!" she begged. "My brothers and I need you. Please, listen!"

She told him their story and all that Aoife had said.

"You are safe now," said the man when he heard. "That was the sound of holy Patrick's bell. I will take care of you for the rest of your days."

The good man kept his word. He fed the swans and made them a cosy nest. Night after night he listened as they told him of times long gone and all that had happened since. Then, one day, as he reached out to touch them, their feathers fell away. Finnuala and her brothers were human again. They were nine hundred years old. The good man had scarcely blessed them when they died. Tenderly he buried them in one grave.

That night five stars swooped across the glittering sky. He knew then that Lir and his children were together again, in some beautiful, far-off place ...

THE GIANT'S CAUSEWAY

Fionn Mac Cumhail was very pleased with himself. He was taking a little gentle exercise – jumping over trees, diving from mountain-tops, smashing great stones with his bare hands.

"Ooooh, Fionn!" giggled the women, "you're wonderful, so strong and brave and handsome!"

Fionn swaggered and smiled.

"It's nothing!" he said. "I just like to keep myself fit, that's all."

His wife, Bláithín, didn't like it.

"You're always bragging and boasting," she said to him. "Some day it will land you in big trouble."

Fionn laughed.

"Don't be daft," he said. "Don't you know – I'm strong and brave and handsome! Now give me a kiss for I'm off to Antrim. Myself and the Fianna are building a bridge to Scotland. There are giants over there that I'm longing to conquer."

Bláithín sighed, but kissed him tenderly.

Fionn was in cheerful mood as he set off for Antrim. It was a pleasant walk. Haws reddened the hedges, sunlight dappled the sleepy glens. He felt so happy that he could not help singing a little tune:

"Fol the dol day ro,
  only a fool
  would dare pick a fight
  with the bold Fionn Mac Cumhail!"

It sounded so good that he sang it over and over.

In no time at all, Fionn and the Fianna were in Antrim. They never stopped till the blue-green swish of the sea rolled restlessly before them.

Building the bridge was play to Fionn. He worked quickly and easily, splitting the stones into splendid pillars and columns. Further and further they stretched out into the ocean.

Now and again he thought of what the women said and wandered over to a rock pool to look at himself. Yes, it was true – he was strong and brave and handsome. Around him the Fianna were respectfully silent as he sang his song:

"Fol the dol day ro,
  only a fool
  would dare pick a fight
  with the bold Fionn Mac Cumhail!"

From time to time, there came a distant rumble.

"Is it thunder?" asked the Fianna, but they went on working. Then one of their spies came ashore, tired and gasping.

"I've just been to Scotland!" he said. "There's a huge giant there called Fathach Mór. He's doing long jumps in the Highlands – you can hear the thumping!"

"How big is he?" asked Fionn.

"His shadow stretched all across the Highlands," the spy replied.

'Hmmm,' thought Fionn, 'that big! Maybe this bridge is not such a good idea after all.'

But he could not admit that he was nervous so he kept on building.

A few days later, there came a distant whistling.

"Is it the wind?" asked the Fianna, but they kept on working.

Just then another spy came ashore, stuttering and trembling.

"You won't believe what I've seen!" he stammered. "It's the giant Fathach Mór – he has a magic little finger with the strength of ten men! He's in training for the long jump to Antrim – you can hear him whistling!"

Fionn's face paled.

"The strength of ten men!" he thought. "I'll never fight him. What will I do? He'll squash me into a pancake!"

But he could not admit that he was

nervous, so he said to the Fianna, "I've just had a message from Bláithín. I must go home at once – you can all take a holiday."

He set off by himself and never did a man travel faster through the glens of Antrim. There was no mention now of "Fol the dol day ro". He shook with fear at every footstep, thinking he heard a mighty breath behind him. But it was only the North Wind practising for the winter ...

Bláithín was surprised to see him.

"You're welcome!" she cried, kissing him. "And is the great causeway finished already?"

"No indeed," replied Fionn, "but I couldn't bear to leave you for so long."

Bláithín was delighted. She roasted a leg of venison in celebration – but Fionn didn't eat any. When night came, he kept sitting up in bed, listening.

He couldn't fool Bláithín.

"Fionn Mac Cumhail," she said, "I've known you for a long time. It was more than love for me that brought you home in such a hurry. Now, out with it! What's the matter?"

So Fionn told her.

"What will I do, Bláithín?" he asked. "There's the strength of ten men in his magic little finger. He'll squash me into a jelly!"

Bláithín laughed.

"Is that all that's troubling you?" she asked. "Just leave him to me – I'm well able for any man!"

She got out of bed and sat by the fire, twisting her plaits with her finger. At last she smiled.

"Get up, Fionn," she said. "Stoke up the fire and fetch me the sack of flour. Then go outside and find nine flat stones."

Fionn did as he was told, though she wouldn't reveal her plan.

She worked all night making ten oatcakes. In each she put a large flat stone, all except the last. This one she marked with her thumbprint.

It was dawn now and the house floated with the smell of baking. Bláithín turned to Fionn.

"Go and cut down some wood," she said. "You must make an enormous cradle."

Fionn worked all morning, smoothing and shaping. The cradle was just finished when there was a mighty rumble and the dishes shook on the dresser!

"It's him!" squealed Fionn.

"Don't worry!" said Bláithín. "Put on this bonnet. Now into the cradle and leave me to do the talking."

Fionn was scarcely ready when a knock outside set the house rattling. Bláithín opened the door, but all she could see was a pair of knees.

"Does Fionn Mac Cumhail live here?" boomed a great voice above her.

"He does," said Bláithín, "though he's away at the moment. He's gone to capture the giant, Fathach Mór."

"I'm Fathach Mór!" bellowed the giant. "I've been searching for Fionn everywhere and I've come to kill him."

Bláithín laughed. "Did you ever see Fionn?" she asked. "Sure you're only a baby compared with him! He'll be home shortly and you can see for yourself. But now that you're here, would you do me a favour?"

"What is it?" asked the giant.

"The wind is from the east today," said Bláithín, "and it's blowing straight in the door. Could you turn the house around – I forgot to ask Fionn."

"Certainly," said Fathach Mór, as he spun the house with his little finger.

Fionn gulped and Bláithín's plaits trembled, but she merely smiled.

"Thank you," she said. "Now I've one more thing to ask. The well has run dry and Fionn was supposed to lift up the mountain this morning. There's spring water underneath it. Do you think you could get me some?"

"Of course," shouted the giant as he scooped out a hole in the mountain, the size of a crater.

Fionn shook with fear in the cradle and even Bláithín turned pale. But she thanked the giant graciously and invited him in.

Stooping and grunting, he struggled through the door. The earth shook, mugs and platters clattered to the floor. Bláithín wiped a chair for him and set it by the table.

"Though you and Fionn are enemies, you are still a guest," she said. "Have some fresh bread." And she put the oatcakes before him.

Fathach Mór began to eat. Almost at once he gave a piercing yell and spat out two teeth.

"What kind of bread is this?" he screeched. "I've broken my teeth on it!"

"I'm sorry about that," Bláithín said. "Fionn always eats it!"

Hearing this, the giant took another bite.

"Blood and thunder!" he roared. "There's two more gone! Those cakes are as hard as stone!"

"How can you say such a thing?" asked Bláithín. "Even the child in the cradle eats them!" And she gave Fionn the cake with the thumbprint.

"Goo gaa gaa," gurgled Fionn, eating every crumb.

For the first time, Fathach Mór looked at the cradle.

"Whose child is that?" he asked in wonder.

"That's Fionn's son," said Bláithín.

The giant was silent for a moment.

"And how old is he?" he asked then.

"Just ten months," replied Bláithín. "He's a fine healthy lad. When he grows up, he'll be just like his dad."

"Can he talk?" asked the giant.

"Not yet, but you should hear him roar! Fionn can't bear to hear him. He'd kill anyone who upsets him."

At once, Fionn began to yell.

"Quick, quick!" cried Bláithín. "Let him suck your little finger. If Fionn comes home and hears him, he'll be in such a temper."

With an anxious glance at the door, the giant gave Fionn his finger to suck.

Crinch! Crunch! Snap! Fionn cracked his teeth through the bone and bit off the giant's magic little finger!

"AAAAAAAAHHHHHHHH !!!!!!!" screamed the giant as he slithered to the floor. Screeching and roaring, he bolted from the house.

Fionn leaped from the cradle in bib and bonnet and danced his Bláithín round the kitchen.

❖

The Giant's Causeway was never finished. It stands there to this day, its huge stepping-stones stretching towards Scotland. And maybe Fathach Mór wanders there still, crying and moaning and screeching for his finger. But it's probably just the North Wind practising for the winter ...

THE BODACH OF THE GREY COAT

"Fionn, Fionn, come quickly – there's someone to see you!"

Fionn groaned. He had just been enjoying an afternoon snooze and didn't feel like visitors. He stretched himself and yawned.

A foreign ship floated in the bay and along the beach strode a stranger. He was dark-skinned and handsome, with gorgeous clothes and a richly jewelled sword.

"Who are you and where do you come from?" asked Fionn.

"My name is Caol an Iarainn, Prince of Greece," the stranger replied, "though my name in Greek is a much finer one."

"And what is your business?" asked Fionn pleasantly.

"I have come to conquer your finest soldier," said the prince. "I will be king then, and all your people will pay me taxes."

Fionn laughed.

"I'm afraid you'll be disappointed," he said. "I've never met a man yet who could beat any of my soldiers."

"You're a fool to talk like that!" snapped Caol an Iarainn. "Not one of you could defeat me. But I'll have mercy on you – if I lose, I'll return to Greece and that's the last you'll hear of me."

"It's a bargain!" declared Fionn. "Now what test of skill shall we decide on?"

"You may please yourself," replied the prince. "I am champion of Greece in fighting, wrestling and running."

"Let us settle on running," Fionn said. "Our best runner is at the High King's fort in Tara, but I'll fetch him here myself."

Fionn set off at once. He was not too worried about the cocky prince. After all, his best runner darted like an arrow ... He whistled merrily as he strode through the woods.

Suddenly he halted. Something rustled in the trees. What was it? A deer? A boar? Fionn waited. A tall, skinny man stepped out before him. His scruffy grey coat was spattered with dirt. Mud plastered the hem and sticking out from under it was a pair of enormous feet. Each shoe was the size of a boat, and at every step a slather of mud squelched around him.

Fionn was so surprised that he couldn't speak. But the man didn't seem to notice. "Good day to you, Fionn Mac Cumhail," he said cheerfully, "and how are you this beautiful autumn evening?"

"How do you know my name?" asked Fionn.

"Oh, everyone knows the great Fionn Mac Cumhail, leader of the Fianna," replied the creature.

"And who are you?" asked Fionn.

"I am someone and no one," replied the man. "I'm not much to look at but I can run like the wind."

"How strange!" cried Fionn, and he told the story of the prince from Greece.

The man looked serious.

"I know this fellow you speak of," he said, "and he's quite right – not even your best runner could beat him. But don't worry, I'll be your runner! Leave him to me. I'll give him a race to remember!"

Fionn looked doubtful. Could he really trust this man? He didn't even know his name, though Bodach seemed to suit him. People often used this name for someone clumsy and dirty.

Should he keep going on to Tara for his own man? He thought of the handsome prince with his haughty face and perfect clothes. Suddenly, he grinned.

"Right!" he said. "You shall run for the Fianna, though how you don't trip in those huge shoes is a mystery!"

They returned to the beach before the sun went down. Caol an Iarainn was waiting with his servants.

"Here is your rival," Fionn said.

Caol an Iarainn looked the Bodach up and down.

"I am a king's son!" he gasped. "Do you expect me to race against that ... that ... thing?"

All the Fianna burst out laughing.

"Nobody laughs at me!" he screeched. "I will race this fool tomorrow. Then you will be my slaves and I will have your kingdom!"

"Well," said the Bodach to the prince, "we'd better find shelter for the night. Will you help me build a hut to sleep in?"

"I will not!" snapped Caol an Iarainn. "My servants will hang a hammock for me in the woods."

"Very well," said the Bodach, "I will build one myself."

In no time at all, he had woven a hut together.

"Caol an Iarainn," he said then, "will you help me hunt for some food?"

"I will not!" snarled Caol an Iarainn. "My servants will feed me with the best meats."

"Very well," said the Bodach, "I will go hunting myself."

Soon he returned from the woods with a wild boar which he roasted over a fire. Then, folding his cloak about him, he curled up to sleep. So strong were his snores that the ground shook, and Caol an Iarainn spent the night falling out of his hammock.

Dawn came. The eastern light fell on Caol an Iarainn's face and woke him. He was cranky and tired after his disturbed night. He stepped across to the Bodach's hut to find him still sleeping. Not wishing to be called a cheat, Caol an Iarainn woke him.

"It's time for the race to begin," he said.

The Bodach rubbed his eyes.

"It's scarcely morning," he said, "and I'm not finished sleeping.

You go ahead – I'll catch up with you later." And, rolling over, he was soon snoring again.

'This man is a fool!' thought Caol an Iarainn to himself as he set off running.

An hour later, the Bodach awoke. He finished off the roast boar and, wrapping the bones in his coat, off he went.

In no time he had caught up with Caol an Iarainn. "You look tired already!" he called as he darted past. "Did you not sleep well? Never mind, here are some bones to chew on." And he threw them to the prince.

"I don't need your rubbish!" yelled Caol an Iarainn furiously. But the Bodach was already out of sight.

On went the Bodach through bog and forest. It was now almost midday and he was hot and thirsty. Away to the left swept a wild rough valley, knitted and knotted with bush and briar. Clusters of blackberries glistened in the sunlight. The Bodach halted and tore them off in

bunches. Then, leaning against a rock, he ate till he was satisfied.

Along came Caol an Iarainn.

"Your coat is torn!" he called as he hurried past. "There's a piece of it caught in some thorns beyond the last mountain!"

The Bodach looked down to see a large hole.

"So it is!" he said. "I must go back." And he turned around at once.

"What a fool that man is!" laughed the prince to himself as he galloped into the distance.

An hour passed before the Bodach found the missing piece of cloth. He sat down on a tree stump and sewed it back on. Then, lazily stretching himself, he set off on the race again.

He soon caught up with Caol an Iarainn.

"You'd better hurry!" he called cheekily as he trotted past.

Caol an Iarainn was raging. He forced himself to run even faster but the Bodach was already far ahead.

Evening came and the Bodach was hungry again. Eventually, he saw another clump of blackberries – bigger and juicier than he had ever eaten. He stuffed himself till his hands and face were dark with their juice. Taking off his coat, he filled it up with millions of blackberries – he could not bear to leave the remainder. Then, throwing the load over his shoulder, he set off again.

The sun was setting. It rippled in golden frills across the ocean. Fionn was getting restless. He sent out a scout to see if the runners were coming. The scout returned, breathless and frightened.

"I see a dark man approaching!" he gasped. "He's still running and there's a great grey bundle on his shoulder!"

"It's Caol an Iarainn," Fionn groaned. "Only he has such dark skin. He must have killed the Bodach and carries the dead body on his shoulder!"

The Fianna were filled with gloom. They had liked the cheerful, scruffy stranger. Now he was dead and all their kingdom was in the hands of a foreigner ...

At that moment the dark man trotted into the camp.

"Why are you all so sad?" he asked. "Give me a drink quickly and some meal to mix with these delicious blackberries." And he threw his coat full of fruit on the floor.

How the Fianna laughed at the scout's mistake! The Bodach was indeed as dark as the prince – from eating blackberries!

Seconds later Caol an Iarainn came storming in.

"You cheat!" he screamed, lunging forward with his sword.

In a flash, the Bodach snatched a ball of blackberry mash and flung it at the prince. The blow was so hard that Caol an Iarainn's head was turned back to front. The Bodach picked him up by one leg and ran

outside. Then, leaning over the cliff, he dropped the king's son, head first into his ship.

"Caol an Iarainn!" he roared, "the Fianna will spare your life. But you must promise to send Fionn Mac Cumhail every penny of taxes collected in Greece from this day on!"

"I promise!" blubbered the prince.

Then the Bodach kicked Caol an Iarainn's ship with his enormous shoe – and sent it twenty leagues in one sweep!

Fionn and the Fianna clapped and cheered. But all of a sudden a mighty wind whirled around them. There was a clap of thunder and a swirling bubble of light. The Bodach was transformed! He was no longer a scruffy stranger but Manannán Mac Lir, the sea-god. He had come to help the Fianna in their hour of need.

With great joy they prepared a splendid feast. It went on for days and everyone ate three bowls each of the wonderful blackberries.

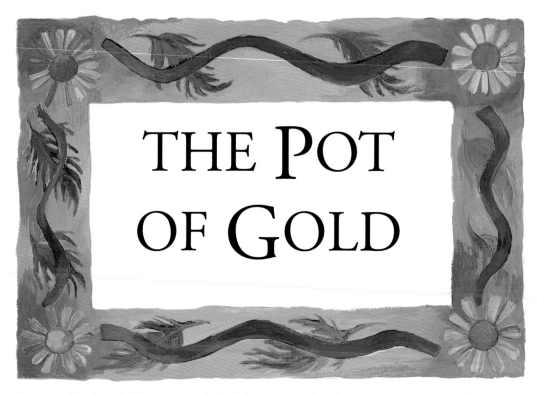

THE POT OF GOLD

Dan Kelly lived alone. He didn't have a wife, for no girl would marry him. He was lazy and untidy. Not for him the hard work and neat farms of his neighbours. His fields were full of weeds, gates sagged, his cattle rambled the roads. Dan preferred to spend his time dreaming. He had great plans: one day he would be rich and have everything he could wish for. Some bit of luck was sure to happen ...

This morning though, he was up early. It was a feast day and there would be sports and dancing in Ballycahill. He put on his only suit, then reached for a tie – his best red silk one. A flick of the comb and he was ready.

It was a long walk to Ballycahill. At first the road passed along by his own farm. It didn't bother him that the neighbours' fields teemed with full ripe crops of oats and barley. There they were – poor things – slaving away while he was off on a day's outing.

Clouds of dust flurried his shoes as he walked, then a shoelace loosened. He stooped to tie it.

"Tic! Tac! Tic!"

What was that noise in the field beside him? Puzzled, he listened.

"Tic! Tac! Tic!"

Was it a grasshopper? No, this was louder and sharper. Was it a thrush, smashing a snail's shell against a stone? No, this was completely different.

On tiptoe, Dan peered through the hedge. What he saw almost caused him to stumble into the briars. There in the field sat the

smallest man you could imagine. His hat was red with a white feather in it, and he wore a little leather apron. A leprechaun!

Dan gave a great big grin. Here surely was the bit of luck he had been waiting for. Straightening his tie, he clambered clumsily through the hedge. There was a loud rrrriiiippppp on the seat of his pants – but what harm? Soon he would be buying a new suit ...

The leprechaun looked up as Dan stepped into the field.

"Good morning, Dan," he said. "Are you going to the fair of Ballycahill?"

"I was on my way," said Dan, "when I heard you working, so I thought I'd stop for a minute."

"You're very welcome," said the leprechaun politely. "Sit down and rest yourself. There's a rock there behind you."

Dan was just about to turn when he remembered – if he looked away even for a second, the leprechaun would vanish.

'He's a crafty little fellow,' thought Dan. 'I'll have to be careful.' So he just stood where he was.

"That's a grand little shoe you're making," he said.

"It is indeed," said the leprechaun. "There's a big ball tonight in Liosachoill. It's a pair of dancing shoes for the Queen of the Fairies."

Dan had never seen anything so lovely.

"They're gorgeous," he said, "but it isn't shoes I'm looking for."

"I didn't think it was," sighed the leprechaun.

"No indeed," said Dan, "I'm after your pot of gold. Everyone knows that leprechauns have loads of money."

"Pot of gold?" laughed the leprechaun. "You must be joking! Why do you think I'm sitting here working, while the rest of the world is feasting and merrymaking?"

"Your world isn't my world," said Dan, "and why you're working is none of my business. But it's my field you're sitting in and I want the gold this instant!"

"And a poor bit of a field it is too!" remarked the leprechaun. "Look at it – full of poisonous ragwort, and all the seeds blowing in on your neighbours. Aren't you ashamed of yourself?"

"The gold!" screeched Dan in a terrible temper. He'd heard plenty of complaints about his fields already. "The gold – get me the pot of gold!" And he snatched the little man in a vicious grip.

"Let me go!" squealed the leprechaun. "I'm meeting in the middle! You have the breath squeezed out of me!"

"I'll let you go when you show me where the pot of gold is!" roared Dan.

"All right! I'll show you!" croaked the leprechaun. "Just put me down!"

Dan dropped him roughly on to the grass. With his hat squashed

sideways, the leprechaun hopped across to a clump of ragwort. "It's under here," he said sulkily.

Dan groaned. He had no spade and the field was dotted with ten thousand clumps of ragwort. Sweat ran down his face and he loosened his collar. At once an idea came to him. He grinned, then taking off his tie, he knotted it round the piece of ragwort.

"I'm going home for a spade," he said to the leprechaun. "Will you promise me on your honour that you will not touch that tie?"

"I promise," said the leprechaun.

For a lazy man, Dan Kelly could move very quickly. In minutes he was home and back again. But when he reached the field, the spade clattered from his hand. The leprechaun was gone and red ties fluttered cheerfully on ten thousand clumps of ragwort ...

Dan Kelly didn't go to the fair that day. He spent the afternoon sewing the seat of his trousers. Once or twice he thought he heard someone laughing, but it was only the wind in the chimney. He never did buy another suit, but he had plenty of ties to wear to the fair of Ballycahill ...

TÍR NA n-ÓG

Far away, in the land of Tír na n-Óg, there lived a king. Every seven years there was a race from the fort gates to the top of a steep hill. First to reach the throne on the hilltop was made king. Three times he had won the race, but now he was getting nervous.

One day he sent for the chief druid.

"I am worried that someone else will win the next race," said the king. "Then I would be king no longer."

"Don't worry," replied the chief druid, "you are easily the fastest runner. The only person who will ever defeat you is the man your daughter will marry."

"What?" roared the king.

He thought of his only daughter, Niamh, who was so beautiful that every man who saw her fell madly in love with her. It was only a matter of time before she married. The king was furious.

"She will never marry!" he roared. "You must cast a spell on her that will make her ugly and disgusting."

"I cannot do such a thing," answered the chief druid, "I have known Niamh since she was born."

"And so have I," snarled the king. "But not even my own daughter will cause me to lose my crown!"

Then, snatching the chief druid's magic stick, he strode into the garden. With one touch his daughter's head became a pig's!

"Now," raged the king, "no one will ever marry you and I will rule for ever."

Poor Niamh! She ran to her room, screaming and sobbing. She could not believe that her father had done such a thing. What would become of her? Would she ever be an ordinary girl again?

One morning the chief druid came to visit her.

"Oh, Niamh," he said, "if only I could undo the harm your father has done!"

"Then help me, please!" cried Niamh. "Surely you can do something."

"There is only one way to get rid of this wicked spell," the chief druid explained.

"You must marry one of the sons of Fionn Mac Cumhail. If you succeed, the pig's head will disappear."

"But who would ever marry me as I am?" cried Niamh.

"I'm sorry," said the druid, "there is nothing else I can do."

All that day, Niamh thought of what the chief druid had said. At last she made up her mind. When darkness came she dressed herself in a long hooded cloak. Then, taking her white horse, she set off for Ireland. Over the sea went the wonderful white horse, his hooves scarcely touching the water. Dawn mist shimmered as they reached the shore.

It did not take Niamh long to find Fionn Mac Cumhail and his sons. The forests rang with the shouts of their hunting and the nights echoed with their songs. One of Fionn's sons was named Oisín. He was strong and handsome, swift on his feet and fearless in battle. But he was also kind and gentle. Niamh watched from a distance as he rescued a trapped fawn.

'That is the only man I would marry,' she thought. 'But he is so handsome! Every woman in Ireland must be in love with him. What chance have I?'

But Niamh was desperate. Silently she followed Oisín everywhere, keeping in the shadows and never showing her face. One evening, after a good day's hunting, the Fianna went home. Oisín was left alone. He had so much to carry that he could not manage it all. Niamh darted out from the trees.

"Let me help you," she said. The sinking sun rested on her pig's head, and she almost turned and ran.

But Oisín just said, "Thank you, I have too much to carry alone."

They walked a long way. Oisín told her the names of the flowers and birds. At last they stopped to rest. The day was hot and, as Niamh took off her cloak, Oisín looked at her.

"You are very beautiful," he said, "except for the pig's head. How did it happen?"

Slowly, sadly, Niamh told him her story. Tears ran down her ugly face as she remembered her father's treachery.

"The only way I can become completely human is by marrying one of the sons of Fionn Mac Cumhail," she said.

"Is that all it takes?" laughed Oisín. "That's no problem! I am Oisín, son of Fionn, and I will marry you myself."

They were married at once. Gradually the pig's head disappeared and there was the real Niamh — eyes green as the sea, clouds of golden hair hanging to her waist. A band of diamonds glittered on her forehead and her dress shimmered with pearls. Oisín could not speak.

Out of the shadows came Niamh's faithful horse. Silver tassels hung from the polished saddle, beads of rubies dangled from the reins. But Oisín scarcely noticed. He could not take his eyes off this beautiful girl.

"I will never leave you," he said. "I will follow you to the ends of the earth."

"Then get up on my white horse," replied Niamh, "and come with me to Tír na n-Óg. There you will never grow old. You will be young and handsome for ever and have everything you could ask for. There the days sparkle with sunlight and the nights are never cold."

In a daze of love, Oisín mounted the horse. At once they set off, over mountains, rivers and rocks. Soon they came to the ocean. The white horse never stopped, his feet scarcely touching the waves as they crossed. Oisín barely noticed the wonderful places they passed: the water cities, the palaces of light. His face was buried in Niamh's gorgeous hair as it billowed around her. He no longer remembered who he was or what he had left behind ...

When they reached Tír na n-Óg, the king was overjoyed. Many and many a time he had wept for the evil he had brought on his daughter. Now, when he saw her, he begged her forgiveness.

"All my kingdom is yours," he said. "You and your husband will rule for ever."

So Oisín and Niamh began their life together in Tír na n-Óg. They fished in crystal waters, went swimming in warm lakes. They raced their horses on the sparkling beach, feasted on honey and fruit. Oisín made songs for Niamh as they wandered under the stars.

They were the happiest of lovers and Oisín had all he could wish for.

But though Oisín had forgotten his past life, it sometimes came back in his dreams. Then he was with Fionn, his father, and all his brothers and friends. They laughed and joked or hunted with reckless speed. Oisín would wake up then and cry out in grief, for all the loved faces had vanished and were lost in his dreams.

Early one morning Oisín said to Niamh, "It's no good, each day I remember more and more. I must go back to Ireland to see my father and friends."

"There's nothing to go back for," Niamh said. "You have been in Tír na n-Óg for three centuries. Your father and friends are all dead and gone."

"Nonsense!" laughed Oisín. "I've only been here a few years. I must go, Niamh, just for a day. Then I will return and never leave you again."

"Very well," Niamh said, "since I love you I will let you go. Take my white horse, but be very careful. You must not get off the horse. If you do, you will never see me or Tír na n-Óg again."

Then she kissed him tenderly, but her eyes were full of shadows ...

The white horse took Oisín across the sea as before. But though it pranced as lightly as ever, Oisín felt no joy. Clouds smothered the horizon, thunder echoed and died. At last the horse scrambled ashore. It was raining but Oisín didn't care. He thought of his father and friends – how surprised they would be to see him!

Suddenly he paused. Where were the woods he had hunted in? And the river – where were the stepping-stones? A bridge stretched over it, people were coming and going. How puny they looked, and how they stared at him! It was very strange.

"Where can I find Fionn Mac Cumhail?" he asked a girl. But the girl shook her head.

"Never heard of him," she said.

Puzzled and upset, Oisín rode further.

"Where are Fionn Mac Cumhail and his warriors, the Fianna?" he asked a group of men.

They looked at one another and shrugged. Then one old man spoke.

"Fionn and the Fianna? My grandfather used to talk about them. But they're all dead and gone this three hundred years."

Three hundred years! Oisín remembered what Niamh had said. Could it be true? He would go to the Hill of Allen where Fionn had his fort – surely he'd see them there! But the fort was in ruins. Weeds and nettles grew up between the stones.

Oisín was heartbroken. He could not believe that his father and friends were dead.

"I'll go to Tara," he thought, "to the High King himself. Surely there, someone will tell me the truth." He turned the patient horse around and headed north.

Beside the road some men were trying to lift a stone.

"They're so weak!" thought Oisín. "Not even six together can lift it, but I could do it with one hand."

He leaned from the saddle and tossed the stone easily into the cart. The men gasped. But instantly there was a snap! The stirrup broke and Oisín tumbled off the horse. As he hit the ground, Niamh's warning was screaming in his ears – but it was too late. The proud, handsome warrior disappeared and Oisín became a withered old man. The white horse tossed his head and galloped away.

Someone rushed from a nearby hut. It was the holy man, Patrick. Lifting Oisín up in his arms, he carried him inside. For days he nursed him, while Oisín told him of Fionn and the Fianna and the days of long ago.

Then Oisín died.

❖

It was the end of the Fianna, the last great band of heroes and poets. And maybe, too, it was the end of Tír na n-Óg, for Niamh of the golden hair was never seen again ...

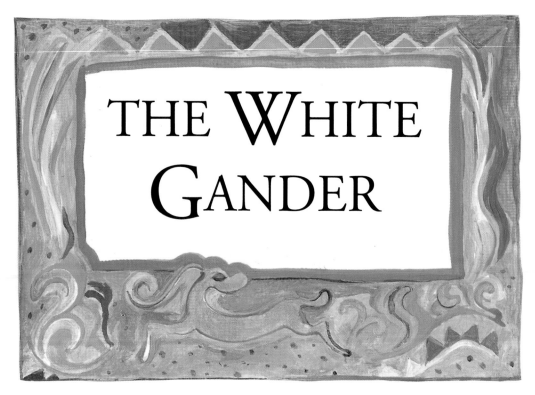

THE WHITE GANDER

In days gone by, there lived a poor widow who had only one son. His name was Séamas and he was the laziest, most foolish lad you could imagine. Every morning his mother got up early to milk the cows and light the fire and bring water from the well. But Séamas lay in bed till midday. He spent his days wandering the fields, talking to himself and making poems in his head.

When night came, he might take down the old uilleann pipes that once belonged to his father. Though the old man had been a famous piper, lazy Séamas only ever bothered to learn one tune. However, as there was a great shortage of musicians at the time, Séamas was invited to every feast and funeral.

One Hallowe'en night, there was a dance in the next valley. Word came for Séamas to go over. He washed and shaved, making every 'Oooh' and 'Aaah' at himself in the spotted mirror.

"Now Séamas, a ghrá," said his mother, "don't let any girls be making eyes at you. And mind you don't be drinking whiskey for fear you'd fall in a bog-hole. And there'll be fresh soda bread waiting for you when you get home."

He set off. The moon hung low and the road was polished with light. He didn't mind the odd shapes of briar and branch or the wind that hummed in the hawthorn bushes. Neither did he notice the shadow that stepped behind him, though it wasn't his. On he went, thinking only of the welcome and the warm fire that awaited him.

When Séamas reached the house, all was as expected. There was a cheer and a clap as he pushed in the half-door. He was brought straight to the hearth to warm himself. The dancers were ready and eager, and never mind that he could only play one tune.

The night flew past. Between dances they had snap-apple and ducking, and toasted barm brack. At last it was time to go. The people of the house came with him to the door.

"Safe home now, Séamas," they said, "and mind the Púca!"

The Púca was a spirit that was said to roam on Hallowe'en night. It was thought to be something half-way between a horse and a goat. It spat on blackberries and all wild fruits, so no one could eat them after that.

Séamas was not thinking of the Púca as he set off home. He was thinking of the fresh milk and soda bread his mother would have left for him. He was thinking of his cosy bed by the fire and how you could lie

there listening to the crickets on the hearth. He was thinking that he would wait in bed in the morning and his mother might bring him tea in the bed when she had finished milking ...

The road seemed long and Séamas was very tired. When he got to Clooncouse bridge he stopped to rest. He dropped his pipes on the grass and leaned over to look in at the water. The moon shimmered up at him. It made him dizzy to look at the gold of it coming and going and breaking and joining up again. He shook his head as he stooped for his pipes.

"Can you play 'The White Gander'?" asked a voice behind him.

Séamas nearly dropped dead with fright for he could see no one. Then out of the shadows stepped a strange creature. It looked like a horse but there were two curling horns on its head. Séamas knew at once that it was the Púca.

"Can you play 'The White Gander'?" said the Púca again.

"'Th ... th ... the White Gander'?" stuttered Séamas. "I ... I never heard of it!"

"Come here," said the Púca, "and I'll teach it to you."

But Séamas couldn't move hand or foot with the fright.

Over stepped the Púca and poked him with his horns.

"Now play!" he said.

Séamas put the pipes to his elbow, though he knew well that he had only the one tune and that wasn't 'The White Gander'. To his great surprise a roll of notes came pouring from the pipes, clearer and sweeter than any he had ever heard. His fingers flew of their own accord while the music soared over the fields and away into the night. Children smiled in their sleep and old people dreamed themselves young again.

"That's powerful music!" said the Púca. "And I know who'd love to hear it. Come with me now and you'll be richly rewarded."

Before Séamas could speak, he found himself on the Púca's back and clattering along the road. With one hand he clutched the Púca's shaggy hair while with the other he clung tightly to his pipes. Faster and faster they went, swerving in across the bogs. They galloped over streams and through woods. Once a fox crossed their path. Séamas saw his red, frightened eyes but they were not nearly so frightened as his own.

Now they were up and away above the earth. Higher and higher they soared. Below him Séamas saw the sleepy town and the top of the church steeple. Wind whisked his ears and billowed his jacket out behind him. Once he nearly slid off and made a frantic grab to steady himself. He cried out with terror but the Púca chuckled.

"Hold on to your pipes, Séamas," he said. "We're nearly there."

"But ... but where are we going?" Séamas asked.

"To the top of Knocknashee, the fairy mountain," said the Púca. "The fairy host is waiting. They always have a party on Hallowe'en night.".

Séamas groaned. 'I'll never see my mother again,' he thought. 'When the fairies get hold of you, they never let you go.'

The mountain loomed before them.

"We're going to crash!" he gasped.

But the Púca only laughed and landed lightly on his feet. Séamas tumbled head first into a clump of heather.

There was no house to be seen, not a candle or lamp.

"Where's the party?" asked Séamas, getting stiffly to his feet.

The Púca didn't say a word but tapped with his horns on a huge slab of rock. Immediately it opened into a hollow of soft golden light.

"Follow me," said the Púca.

He trotted down a long passage and into a great hall. A thousand

lamps sparkled on the walls. Arches and stairs of polished marble swept over a glass floor. In the centre stood a great table – and there sat a hundred old hags.

Séamas had never seen anything so ugly in his life. Their skin was creased and drooping, their hair matted and grey. Some had no teeth, and others had animals' claws for nails. But they grinned at Séamas as he walked down the hall.

"I have brought you the best piper in Ireland!" said the Púca. "Now give him food and drink."

Séamas looked at the food – cakes light as sea foam, drinks sparkling with bubbles ... But though he longed for a taste, he shook his head.

"No, thanks," he said. "I'm not hungry."

He remembered in time what his mother always said: if once you eat or drink in the fairy world, you will never return home.

One old hag stamped her foot.

"A chair for the piper!" she called. "Let the dancing begin!"

A door opened and in walked a white gander carrying a chair!

"Music, Séamas!" cried the Púca.

The gander began to squawk and screech, and Séamas began to play.

He wondered what would happen when they found out that he had
only one tune ...

He need not have worried. After the tune came 'The White Gander',
then 'The Waves of Tory' and 'The Stack of Barley' and 'The Bridge of
Athlone' and 'The Siege of Ennis'. On and on he played, each tune
sweeter and livelier than the last. He could not understand it.

Séamas played for hours. His fingers dashed and his elbow flew and
his eyes popped in his head. Round and round the hags went whirling.
Their long grey hair flew out behind them, their black skirts swirled.
They shuffled and twisted and battered and stepped – backwards and
forwards and in and out in fours and sixes and eights. All night long
they danced while Séamas played.

At last they were tired – but Séamas could not stop playing. Faster
and faster went the music, wilder and wilder the dance. They whirled
around in one gigantic circle until all was blurred in a mad hectic swirl.

Suddenly the white gander charged over and
pierced a hole in the pipes!

"Whooooooooooosh!" All the air
came rushing out and the pipes
fell silent.

Séamas mopped his forehead.

"If the gander didn't stop you,"
said a voice, "we would have
danced till we all dropped dead."

Séamas blinked and shook his
head. All the old hags were gone and
in their place stood a hundred beautiful
girls with shining hair and skirts like

rainbows. Smiling and laughing, they gathered around Séamas.

"Your music made us young again," they said. "We are very grateful. We are sorry about your pipes but the white gander has another set for you. They are the best pipes in the country. Now here's payment for your hard night's work." And they each gave him a gold coin.

Before Séamas had time to say "Thank you" he was up on the Púca's back. Once more they whirled through the night and only stopped when they reached Clooncouse bridge. Séamas turned to say goodbye to the Púca, but he wasn't there. Only a wisp of mist shimmered over the river and disappeared. In the distance, a cock crowed. The sun was coming up.

Séamas walked home, his pockets heavy with gold. Carefully he hung up the set of new pipes. He drank his milk and ate the fresh soda bread. Then he put on the fire, milked the cows and brought water from the well. His mother nearly fainted from shock when he brought her breakfast in bed.

Séamas was never foolish any more. He and his mother had plenty of money. He became the best piper in the land. His favourite tune was 'The White Gander', but he never played it on Hallowe'en night.

SOMETHING ABOUT THE STORIES

✤ HOW CÚCHULAINN GOT HIS NAME

Cúchulainn was one of the greatest heroes in Irish mythology. Tales of the Red Branch Knights are among the earliest known and go back thousands of years in the oral tradition. Forts were the fortified dwellings in which the Celts lived. There are many stories that tell of the bravery and strength of Cúchulainn. He is particularly associated with Ulster. Cúchulainn's statue may be seen in the GPO in Dublin. There are several retellings of how Cúchulainn got his name – this one was told to me when I was a little girl.

✤ THE MAGIC SHOES

The story is based on a tale that belongs to the earliest cycle of Irish folk-tales, which go back at least 2,000 years and probably further. This retelling is based on the story "Eisirt" in *Legends of Ireland* (1955) by J. J. Campbell and various other sources.

✤ DEIRDRE AND THE SONS OF UISNEACH

The story of Deirdre is one of the most sorrowful tales of Ireland. It is also one of the oldest, told and retold for generations. It was written down in *The Book of Leinster* about 1140.

✤ THE KING'S SECRET

The druids were pagan priests who made laws and had magical powers. Boxty is a type of potato bread still commonly made in Ireland. This retelling is based on "Dhá Chluais Chapaill ar Labhraidh Loingseach" from *Sgéalaigheacht Chéitinn*. The stories were collected in written form in the fifteenth century in the *Yellow Book of Lecan* (1416). A similar tale also exists in Greek mythology.

✤ THE CHILDREN OF LIR

This famous story is one of the oldest known in Ireland and goes back at least 2,000 years. The three destinations of the children of Lir are still known and recognised in modern Ireland. This version is retold from "The Fate of the Children of Lyr", collected by Joseph Jacobs in *Celtic Fairy Tales* (1892). There are many different versions.

❖ THE GIANT'S CAUSEWAY

Fionn Mac Cumhail ranks in importance with Cúchulainn, though the tales are thought to be of a slightly more recent era. There are thousands of stories about Fionn and his band of warriors, the Fianna. This story was probably a way of explaining the actual Giant's Causeway in Co. Antrim. It is based on "A Legend of Knockmany" from *Traits and Stories of the Irish Peasantry*, collected by W. Carleton and published in the mid-nineteenth century.

❖ THE BODACH OF THE GREY COAT

This story tells of another of the adventures of Fionn Mac Cumhail. Manannán Mac Lir was the Celtic god of the sea – the Isle of Man was named after him. The story is based on the Gaelic version "Bodach an Chóta Lachtna". It has existed in the oral tradition for approximately 2,000 years.

❖ THE POT OF GOLD

Leprechauns are little people believed to have lived in Ireland long ago. They were usually seen mending a shoe and always had a pot of gold hidden nearby. This story is based on "The Field of the Boliauns", one of a collection from T. Crofton Croker's *Fairy Legends of the South of Ireland* (1825). Boliaun (*buachallán*) is the Gaelic word for ragwort.

❖ TÍR NA N-ÓG

The story of Oisín in the "Land of Youth" is perhaps the most famous of all Irish tales. It marks the end of the days of the Fianna with their pagan gods and the coming of Christianity to Ireland. The story is retold from *Myths and Folklore of Ireland* (1890), edited by Jeremiah Curtin .

❖ THE WHITE GANDER

The uilleann pipes were commonly played in Ireland. They were played with the elbow, the Gaelic word for elbow being *uilleann*. Snap-apple and ducking are still played on Hallowe'en. Barm brack is a type of fruit loaf eaten on the night. The story is retold from several sources, including *Legends from Ireland* (1977), edited by Seán O'Sullivan and taken from the Irish Folklore Archives. It was recorded in Gaelic in 1956.

PRONUNCIATION GUIDE

(Italics indicate emphasis)

a ghrá	uh *ghraw* (soft g)	Iubdán	*Yub*-dawn
Aisling	*Ash*-ling	Knocknashee	*Knock*-na-*shee*
Aodh	Aay	Labhraidh Loingseach	*Low*-ry *Leeng*-shock
Aoife	*Eef*-ah		
Ballycahill	Bally-*ca*'ill	Leabharcham	*Low*-er-cum (*low* to rhyme with 'how')
Bébó	*Bay*-boh		
Bláithín	*Blaw-heen* (equal emphasis)		
		Liosachoill	Liss-a-*cweel*
Bodach	Bud-*och*	Lir	Lurr
Caol an Iarainn	*Quail* un *Eer*-unn	Lough Derravarragh	Loch Derra-*varr*-agh
Clooncouse	Clune-*coose*		
Conor	*Konn*er	Lough Talt	Loch Tollt
Conor Mac Nessa	*Konn*er Mock Nessa	Manannán Mac Lir	*Monn*-an-awn Mock *Lurr*
Cúchulainn	Coo-*cull*-in	Naoise	*Nee*-sheh
Culann	*Cull*-un	Niamh	*Nee*-uv
Deirdre	*Dare*-dra	Oisín	*Ush*-een
Éanna	*Ayo*-na	Púca	*poo*-ka
Eisirt	*Esh*-ert	Séamas	*Shay*-mass
Ennis	*Enn*-is	Setanta	Se-*tan*-tah
Fathach Mór	*Fah*-huc *Moor*	Shane	Shane
Fergus	*Fer*-gus	Tara	*Tah*-ra
Fianna	*Fee*-yunna	Tír na n-Óg	*Teer* nuh *nogue*
Finnuala	Fin-*noo*-la	Tuatha Dé Danann	*Tooa*-ha *Day Donn*-ann
Fionn	Fee-*yun*		
Fionn Mac Cumhail	Fee-*yun* Mock Coo-il	uilleann pipes	*ill*-unn pipes
		Uisneach	*Ush*-nuch ('ch' as in 'loch')
Inish Glora	*Inn*-ish *Glo*-ra